A COLLECTION OF VILLAINY

Edited By Reuben Messer

First published in Great Britain in 2022 by:

Young Writers
Remus House
Coltsfoot Drive
Peterborough
PE2 9BF
Telephone: 01733 890066
Website: www.youngwriters.co.uk

Printed and bound in the UK by BookPrintingUK
Website: www.bookprintinguk.com
YB0501C

FOREWORD

Welcome, Reader!

Come into our lair, there's really nothing to fear. You may have heard bad things about the villains within these pages, but there's more to their stories than you might think...

For our latest competition, Twisted Tales, we challenged secondary school students to write a story in just 100 words that shows us another side to the traditional storybook villain. We asked them to look beyond the evil escapades and tell a story that shows a bad guy or girl in a new light. They were given optional story starters for a spark of inspiration, and could focus on their motivation, back story, or even what they get up to in their downtime!

And that's exactly what the authors in this anthology have done, giving us some unique new insights into those we usually consider the villain of the piece. The result is a thrilling and absorbing collection of stories written in a variety of styles, and it's a testament to the creativity of these young authors.

Here at Young Writers it's our aim to inspire the next generation and instill in them a love of creative writing, and what better way than to see their work in print? The imagination and skill within these pages are proof that we might just be achieving that aim! Congratulations to each of these fantastic authors.

CONTENTS

Dhwani Patel (12)	51
Corey Greenwood (11)	52
Kasey Smith (11)	53
Lucie Youd (11)	54
James Prior (12)	55
Ethan Jones (11)	56
Charlie Patterson (12)	57
Emily Balde (12)	58
Finley Ogden (11)	59
Imogen Siddall (11)	60
Evie Mann (11)	61
Isobe Rose Rowbotham (12)	62
Hallie Sharples (12)	63
Olivia Meehan (12)	64
Molly Neill (12)	65
Ysabel Brook (11)	66
Daniel Hind (11)	67
Callan Atherton (11)	68
Remy Budgeon (11)	69
Grace Bowmer (12)	70
Emily Faulkner (12)	71

Rainham Mark Grammar School, Gillingham

Rhea Gowda (13)	72
William Adams (13)	73
Rhianna Morgan (14)	74
James Martin (14)	75
Phoebe Coulson (14)	76
Henry Gee (14)	77
Sonika Aulakh (14)	78
Oluwadamilola Olatunji (13)	79
Saffron Tyrone (13)	80
Sophie Evans (14)	81
Ellen Passmore-Feast (13)	82
Joshua Abbott (14)	83
Erin Saunders (13)	84
Charles Firth (13)	85
Kieran Crofts (13)	86

The Martin High School, Anstey

Jenny Conyers (13)	87
Aidan O'Donoghue (13)	88
Oscar Jones (12)	89
Poppy Kinton (12)	90
Harrison West (12)	91
Alfie Gray (13)	92
Kye Easingwood (13)	93
Louis Proud (12)	94
Dylan Roberts (12)	95
Thomas Little (13)	96
Ksenija Bolc (13)	97
Alana Mason (12)	98
Austin Willson (13)	99
Olivia West (13)	100
Alexander Down (13)	101
Ryuji Neal (12)	102
Will Shaw (13)	103
Alex Ashfield (12)	104
Evelyn Stott (13)	105
Jessica Wragg (13)	106
Sophie Penhaligon (12)	107
Lily Carter (12)	108
Lillie Sutherington (12)	109
Vanessa Koscielniak (12)	110
Lola Wright (15)	111
Lucas Armstrong (13)	112
Elljay Layshley-Wardhaugh (12)	113
Woody Payne (12)	114
Ayla Ward (13)	115
Harry Butcher (13)	116
Mia Witherington (12)	117
Rohan Verma (13)	118
Abigail Newton (12)	119
Sky Spicer Hadley (12)	120
Dave Muton (12)	121
Harry Jaques (13)	122
Julia Wojtkiewicz (12)	123
Meg Ainge (13)	124
Marley Onions (12)	125
Cassidy Roberts (12)	126
Joseph Quinn (12)	127
Taylor Leuty-Smith (12)	128

Shylah Johnson (12)	129
Daniel Norman (12)	130
Tyler Barclay Wakefield (13)	131
Olivia Hands (13)	132
Archie Lloyd (13)	133
Jess Hodgkinson (13)	134
Gene Wright (12)	135
Freddie Elkington (13)	136
Niall Farrell (12)	137
Grace Sylvester (13)	138
Curtis Blunt (12)	139
Callum Shokar (12)	140
Caitlyn Timson	141

THE STORIES

HERO OR VILLAIN?

The buildings of parliament crumbled around me as Politiguy approached. "Tornado... what did you do?"
"I did what I had to!" I snarled, the glowing nuclear reactor spinning above my head.
"People died because of what you did," he yelled.
"N-No! I helped them. Santica's government were poisoning them! I freed them," I stammered, looking at the bodies strewn across the parking lot.
"That nuclear reactor was their only protection. You destroyed any chance they had," he snapped at me, "Now Cortina has invaded them." I looked at the island across from me. Fires and wreckage had already started.
"No..."

Abi Dowding (18)
Boston High School, Boston

KING OF THE UNDERWORLD

Distraught Hades looked upon the scene before him, Zeus, his own brother torturing Prometheus. He went to say something, get him to stop, anything, but before he could utter a single word Zeus turned to him with an evil grin on his face.

"Well what am I going to do with you?" he smirked. "Can't have you talking now can we?"

"Please don't do anything," Hades begged but before he could do anything, Zeus created a portal sending him to an unknown world which Hades later became the king of, creating the underworld a world of the unseen and dead.

Summer Elise Hallgarth (13)
Boston High School, Boston

TWISTED TALES

I had never intended on being the villain in the story. But here I am, Alex Bateman, helping the League of Villains itself murder and exploit innocent people. For some reason, when I commit these so-called horrible crimes, I don't feel anything. The chains of sympathy and fear don't hold me back, I just break through them so easily. When I come home with bloodied hands and bruised hands, I just smile. But, one day I came home with bruises and scars. Not because I murdered someone, because somebody nearly murdered me. I'm here for revenge, I'm here to kill.

Aristeja Demenyta (11)

Boston High School, Boston

TWISTED TORTURE

Murder. The only way to keep me sane. Hearing the helpless cries become silent is the very purpose of my existence. No one will ever make me bow down to them as they once did. "You devil! How dare you!" Ecstasy filled my heart as I faced a petite girl with swollen eyes burning with resentment. "Do you not feel an ounce of pity for the countless people you have murdered?"

Ignoring the sting from my heart, I step closer; grabbing her throat and smashing her against the wall. "Silence, before I send you to your demise."

Blaize Thattil (14)
Boston High School, Boston

THE UNSEEN

This time there'll be no witness. I lie there in my cold, dark, serene flat. I've committed a few crimes my whole life without getting caught but today's the turning point. "Why would anyone suspect me, an old man who does nothing but good to anyone?" Only one person in the whole city doubts me and in a matter of few minutes he will be taking his last breaths, without any explanation of his untimely death... no evidence, no eye witness, nothing at all. Soon, I will be the city's one and only strength left, I have nothing to fear.

Aadya Valecha (13)
Boston High School, Boston

THE PLAN

I was sitting, plotting my next move. When all of a sudden a woman appeared from the shadows... it was Storm.
"I have to see what you're up to, I'm fed up of you destroying our city," she exclaimed angrily. I grabbed the sheet of paper I wrote my plan on and shoved it in a vase. I couldn't let her see the plan!
"No!" I shouted.
"I will have to do this the hard way," she muttered.
I yelled, "My plan! I can't remember it! This is all your fault!" I cried out. It went pitch-black...

Aimee Salvadori (14)
Boston High School, Boston

THE INEVITABLE

"Saving people might look like fun, but keeping up the image of a hero isn't easy, in fear of one wrong move and you're done for. This is why I have people like you," I explained turning around to it. All I could hear was its panting. It knew its fate; it was going to be stabbed in the back, literally. I didn't give my acquaintance time to retaliate and ended it quickly. Another night gone.
It's not that I can't control myself... it's just that blood is the only drink that can fully quench my thirst.

Simra Naveed Khan (15)
Boston High School, Boston

WORDS OF THE WICKED

I emerged from the shadows, not yet revealing myself to my freshest victim. A small frail woman who sat in the grassy field so entranced by her newest read that she was completely oblivious to what horror awaited her were she to turn her innocent head. Moving so slowly that it seemed time itself had stopped, I slithered ever so slightly closer to the girl. I could hear her breathing now. As if hunter and predator I raised my knife readying for the kill but before I did she turned and I saw her face. She was my wife...

Zuzanna Kotlega (16)
Boston High School, Boston

WHY WAS SHE BAD?

November 1st, 1980, I was just finishing work when my fiance and my one little child came to pick me up. I jumped in the car with joy and kissed my love but little did I know that would be my last ever kiss. We happily drove home when the ground was shuddering, mightily the love of my life stopped the car in a panic. My favourite superhero Vine was stopping her arch-nemesis, she decided to break the road to crush her. A hole began to form in the road, my family died in the hole.

Scarlett Owston (11)
Boston High School, Boston

REDEMPTION

It was time to make it up to him. Jack stepped through the gnarly, oak wardrobe and emerged in a musty, pitch-black room. Out of the darkness appeared two luminescent, black eyes. A candle flickered on somewhere in the room, the shadow of the flames dancing across the walls. The figure was indescribably hideous. The corpse dragged its distorted limbs across the splintered floor. Its face was most hideous of all. Jack could see the distorted skill under the translucent skin, hanging off like a tablecloth. The creature let out a low, gurgling growl. It shrieked and dived towards Jack.

Olly Walpole (13)
Canford School, Canford Magna

AFTER EVER AFTER

I still haven't forgotten the face she gave me. Her hollowed-out eyes ripped into mine and I surveyed her ghastly face. Grime had built up because of the absence of bathing. Small maggots crawled along her oily face. Her lips were cut and bruised from surgical procedures to try and wake her from her sleep. Her rounded ears were mountains jutting out of her misshapen head. Oh, her teeth were yellow and mouldy from years of neglect. Wrinkles formed crisscrossing patterns on her ageing face. The coma had not done the repulsive lady any favours. She was still alive, just.

Jacob Royle
Canford School, Canford Magna

AFTER EVER AFTER

I can never forget the cackle and distortion on the night when he appeared, in the murky crippled shadow that lay there before me. A ghoul-like figure planted his feet in the almost extra-terrestrial neon concrete. A pungent lift of air flooded my nostrils with eye-piercing horror. Getting closer and closer the now weary shadow was drifting closer and closer. I couldn't run as my body was tearing back my singed skin. A feeling trudged down my back like verminous leeches tearing my bones to mince. I thought this could be the end, but the end is never here.

Oli Butler (13)
Canford School, Canford Magna

ORIGINAL SIN

A tormented scream escapes from the blood-filled hole I am afraid to call my mouth, and I watch in horror as I began to spit blood and sinew tearing from muscle and bone until I can't separate between what is me and what isn't, immeasurable pain consuming my every fibre. My once ocean blue eyes are sucked into pools of darkness, each one on a separate side of a blood-filled canyon. As I stare into these pits, a malicious grin begins to form on both sides of my face.

"They'll rue the day they messed with me," I silently whisper.

Clementine Watts (14)

Canford School, Canford Magna

MOTIVATION

I'm unsure what happened, what I did. The world was in shadow, everything overcast. Walking at night had never been a good idea yet I still did it, I was drawn to it. Spooky presences were also not uncommon, but this was different. Then it appeared, gliding, almost skating. A demon, tall with a hideous face. Leering towards me, like I was edible. Fear, that's why I did it, why I struck. A hefty branch became a lance that was then rammed into its smirk. It crumbled into dust leaving me feeling terrible. An emotion of guilt that hasn't left.

Zoë Humphries
Canford School, Canford Magna

DOWNTIME

Within the mists of a vast barren land lay a mysterious tunnel leading to nowhere. As I ventured towards the vast and uninhabited concrete structure, I slowly meandered the tunnel. The dark squelchy grass slowly started to split down the middle. Within a blink of an eye, I started plummeting down through the ground. After seconds of descending, I thundered into the rough gravely floor. When I rose to my feet, I felt that I was enclosed within a metal cage surrounded by goblins. It was like I had been transported to a different world. I was stuck down.

Felix Lock
Canford School, Canford Magna

ORIGIN STORY

Watching - unable to move. Eyes locked. The thing, standing on the other side of the mirror; a cold shudder ran down my spine. A grim smirk grew from ear to ear, as I watched myself as I began to split. Muscles and blood ripping from bone and tendons. Intense pain running through every part of my being. My once timid self, transforming into this monster of the darkness. As I looked at myself, I couldn't help but smile.
"Oh, look what you have become," I smiled. "They are going to regret the day they met me." I laughed.

George Fullman
Canford School, Canford Magna

BEHIND THE SCENES

My plan was in motion after the traumatic events of yesterday when me and my friend witnessed the cruellest, blood-curdling death in the town of Bridport. We knew we had to escape. There was no time to warn others, all we could do was run! As morning rose, we heard them - the screeches of demons. We started running from them, they appeared like men in black drapes but they ran and fought like demons. We ran down the dark infested alleyway hearing screeching behind us. My friend and I attacked it. It killed my friend and suddenly all went dark.

Ragnar Raymond (13)
Canford School, Canford Magna

BEHIND THE SCENES

The pilot of the Caribbean flight was tired. He took a break. Without telling anyone, he decided to go to Britain to enjoy a warm cup of tea. Back in the Caribbean, there were queues everywhere and people began to get angry. The amount of hate that gathered for him became shocking. When the pilot arrived back, he was booed by his customers. He became very upset by it and got very depressed. Even his own family hated him now. After a month he died of disappointment, and everyone regretted what they said. Now he will be remembered forevermore.

Oliver Gildert (13)
Canford School, Canford Magna

ORIGIN STORY

I never really belonged, and it was now I realised that most. The boy slowly approached me, the moonlight reflecting off his pathetic flip knife. In a clumsy movement he lunged, embedding his knife in my stomach. Anger burned inside me. Slowly, I felt my limbs growing, sparks of electricity ripping through my veins. I tore the knife out of my stomach. Instantly, the wound burnt over and healed in just moments. The boy in front of me had frozen. He blinked. And I was behind him. I clasped his cold neck and there was a distant crack. I smiled.

Oscar Ingarfield (14)
Canford School, Canford Magna

WHO'S THE REAL VILLAIN NOW?

That superhero act was all a lie. You finally figured it out. I tried to cover everything up... even wiping some people out. The cold breezy night when everyone was at the 'super fun' prom. Ah yes, I remember. The horror in his face, the shock, the panic. His tears, his freckles, his eyes were as blue as they could be, amazingly innocent. I always liked his charming little smile. I miss him so much. What? Why are you calling me the villain? I did all of this for you. Remember our promise? That we will always be together, forever.

Kurumi Hotta
Canford School, Canford Magna

BEHIND THE SCENES

My plan was in motion. The only task left was to enter the startling room, stood there before me. The only thing that troubled me was the thought of myths. They said anyone who entered the room '24b' could be brutally murdered, left chopped in half, or in pieces, or their vital organs absent. Despite all the fear I possessed, I knocked on the door and it rapidly swung open. A booming voice beckoned me in. As I entered the room, something grabbed my leg. I looked to see who it was but saw red fluid trickling down my leg.

Sienna Fitzpatrick (13)
Canford School, Canford Magna

BEHIND THE SCENES

My plan was in motion. I slowly walked down the dark and gloomy hallway. I walked closer and closer to the light, as if I was walking towards my destiny. As I stepped through the mammoth-like doors, the light simply blinded me. My eyes adjusted and I could slowly recognise my hall. This hall was one of my prized possessions. If you were wondering why it's so special to me, this is where people I despise come and have a little chat with me. By a little chat, I mean torturing and murdering them to teach them a lesson.

Sophie Mburu (13)
Canford School, Canford Magna

AFTER EVER AFTER

I stand in the attic looking around. I feel her presence. My twin is here. Waiting for me to arrive and find her. I am here now, searching for her and I have found her. I see her and she screams and shrieks out words unknown to me. Her rotten body throws itself towards me. My silver blade flashes onto her pungent flesh and she shrieks one last time before crumbling to dust. She whispers, "You did this," as she takes her final breath. I've done it. I brought her to life, and I ended her life. Twice.

Joe Bichard
Canford School, Canford Magna

INSIDE MY HEAD

I was thirteen when I found the hole in the ground. This hole led me to my mind. As I climbed in, a party began with lights flashing. To the right were some glass balls. As I looked in, I could see all my memories. On my left was a cage with two people. They looked exactly like me but one looked evil, and one looked good. They told me about how they were anger and happiness and there were other emotions, but they were the strongest. Anger tricked me and ran out the cage and out of the hole.

Harry Badaway (13)
Canford School, Canford Magna

AFTER EVER AFTER

I still haven't forgotten, the moment I woke up and my whole world was swimming - mess. My life was turned upside down; I don't remember how, I don't remember when I did it, but I did. It is all a vague blur, but I remember enough that I can recall the sheer horror and fear that rattled through me. I remember the trail of putrid clots lining the pristine floor of the landing. I can't believe that I had done it. The hungry monster inside me had finally done it.

Alice de Laszlo (14)
Canford School, Canford Magna

CURSE OR GIFT

I never intended to kill anyone. Nobody understands the curse of a superpower. Nobody understands having power you can't control, an entirely separate conscious being that interrupts your thoughts, drives you insane, refuses to be controlled. Nobody understands being hunted, constantly running. Nobody understands the power's desperate need to survive controls you, obstructs your vision until all you see is red. Survive, survive, survive. Nobody tells you, when the moon sinks and instincts fade, your vision clears and the red remains, you're left with power you don't want, responsibility you can't handle. Blood on your hands. What have I done?

Candida Da Rocha (12)
Fulbrook Middle School, Woburn Sands

THE RISE AND FALL OF HITLER

It was September 1st, 1939 in Berlin Germany. The plan was in motion. Churchill was finally going to find out the truth. As he entered the palace King George was in the dining room. "Hallo," echoed Hitler's voice. He pulled out his Walther p38 and fired it at the King's leg, he collapsed in pain. A shadow moved from behind the curtain. A dozen soldiers surrounded Hitler.

"To the tower!" ordered Sergeant Flowers.

"Off with his head!" said Colonel Buttercup. In the darkness of the tower, they swung their sword but he was gone, a flower in his place.

Jake Day (12)
Fulbrook Middle School, Woburn Sands

DROWNING

As the world around me faded from azure to ebony, I let death gently take my last breath, opening my eyes to the beauty of the other side. My body fell limp in the depths of the river, freeing my spirit from its prison. Death's hand waited patiently for me to take it. As I reached forward, the agonising claws of life wrapped around my neck and dragged me back. Back to the pain and loss we call a gift.
"Please let me go, I can't go back."
"Death can't save you now," it hissed, breathing life into my corpse.

Grace Wendy Glastonbury (13)
Fulbrook Middle School, Woburn Sands

HAPPILY EVER AFTER

Happily ever after? Not for us. Cinderella got hers but what about the 'ugly' stepsisters? After Cindy left, Mother worked us like slaves. Our only use was to marry a prince and make her rich and that was gone. We couldn't ask Cinderella for help as she didn't know, that if not for us, she wouldn't have met the prince. So, we took matters into our own hands... We contacted a witch friend, who sent a poisoned teabag. We knew what to do. We spent the rest of our lives doing whatever we wanted, we got our happily ever after.

Elsa Williams (12)
Fulbrook Middle School, Woburn Sands

THE APPLE

I watched the petty, pale-skinned, weak-minded, little girl as she gracefully took the poisonous apple from my grasp and lifted it to her soft, fresh, red lips. As she took the first bite with no care, I smirked gleefully, waiting for her to fall into a precious deep sleep. Her eyes shut with no hesitation and she turned paler than before and dropped heavily to the floor while my heart took a sense of joy to its centre, knowing that now I would be the fairest, most beautiful and adored woman in the kingdom. The kingdom was mine.

Abigail Ambler (12)
Fulbrook Middle School, Woburn Sands

REVENGE

Inelza Quin is the name. You know people say I'm the villain in those fairy-tale stories. But I'm the hero in my story. People say I shouldn't kill others. Like they think I do it for fun. I'm not that psychotic. I mean I know I'm a serial killer but I do it for revenge to manage my grief. Trying to kill the superhero that murdered my daughter. Not like the public cared. Every time I corner them, they slip right through my fingers. But their time is running out. I plan to get my revenge. One way or another.

Sophia Kemeny Ruff (13)
Fulbrook Middle School, Woburn Sands

PAYBACK

It all started when my parents got killed.
"A mistake!" they shouted. It didn't look like a mistake, I saw the whole thing! Ever since I've been planning my revenge. I was fifteen when it happened, now I'm twenty-four; still single. I'm going to rob them till they are homeless. I'll remove all forms of contact and ship them to a small island in the ocean. I'll be there watching them suffer. I'll give them rice one day, not very much at all. Payback is coming. I loved my parents.

Jacob Soles (11)
Fulbrook Middle School, Woburn Sands

HADES

After the death of the King Titan, my father, my brothers and I chose separate places to rule on earth. Poseidon got the seas, Zeus got the sky, and alas, I got the underworld as there were no good things left. Soon after that, they began to envy me and felt I was too powerful. They cursed me to never leave the underworld and people ask me why I am grumpy. The underworld isn't the best place to be stuck for the whole of eternity but thinking about how I would destroy them always cheers me up.

Tom Okeke (12)
Fulbrook Middle School, Woburn Sands

THE SAVIOUR

She was awake, as she hadn't been in eons, and as she hurried towards the surface her terrible purpose was awakened. Vengeance. For Kartana, revenge was the only thing that mattered. At the surface, her devoted servants awaited. A pity they would die with the rest of her former homeworld. She addressed her servants, "You have been loyal," with cruel eyes. Now was the time for vengeance, the obliteration of Levagacore.
"Levagacore, you will pay for the crimes of your ancestors." Bloodthirsty vengeance was pumping through her system. "I am your cleansing and redemption! I am your saviour!..."

Hope Parker (11)
High Tunstall College Of Science, West Park

ASSASSIN BORN KILLER?

Survival's always been my priority. From the day my own parents sold me into slavery in exchange for their pitiful living. Though I don't remember it I still feel rage boil up inside me whenever I think about it. But I mask indifference, as I was trained to do.

Condition-wise the day's perfect. Calm, windless, silent vibrations warn me to step into my den, lookout and temporarily hide. I watch and wait, soon enough, he arrives and my knife goes hurtling into his back, spraying comically red blood everywhere. Easy kill, easy target. Professional assassins don't feel guilt, do they?

Anna Parker (11)
High Tunstall College Of Science, West Park

HOOK'S ESCAPE

'Twas dark and stormy night, perfect conditions for escaping. At dusk, the crew docked the ship onto shore. Swiftly, I jumped onto the shore and made my way into the forest. Dark shadows loomed over me and rain battered my head. I couldn't stop. I located the lost boys' hideout. Just as planned, they were all asleep and Pan was elsewhere. Swiftly, I found Wendy and carried her off, leaving a ransom note in her place for someone to find. It read, 'Bring the talisman to Skull Rock or else!' While returning to my ship, I heard a clock ticking...

Luke Smart (11)
High Tunstall College Of Science, West Park

A VILLAIN'S ORIGIN

For the longest time, the hero Dawn saved the people of her town from being robbed or murdered, but then a new hero appeared and kept getting to crime scenes before she could even get into her suit. The public began to call this mysterious new hero The Sparrow.

As time went on, Dawn began to grow jealous of The Sparrow and one day she found that a crime was being committed and she thought about the fact she could finally beat him. But when she arrived she assisted in the robbery instead of helping. This proves jealousy changes everyone!

Amy Whitlock (12)
High Tunstall College Of Science, West Park

THE CURSE OF COUNT DRACULA

My stories have been told for thousands of years. Count Dracula, a vicious bloodthirsty monster. Terrorising humans for my own liking. What if I told you that wasn't the case? My story begins when I was a very young man, working in the mines when all of a sudden, I came across a stone so shiny and so breathtaking. As soon as I touched it, *swoosh!* A gust of wind came out of nowhere. I felt different and weird like I had gained power which I had not had before. 'Twas the curse of Count Dracula. Born to kill.

Ashton Moore (11)
High Tunstall College Of Science, West Park

GUNPOINT

The air was cold; the sky was black. Darkness engulfed my car, even though the headlights were on. Frost glistened the windows. I was eight at the time, fiddling with my Rubik's cube on the backseat. Dad was driving the car slowly, being cautious of the ice that paved the road. In the corner of my eye, I saw a glimmer of headlights, much brighter than our own. *Crash!*

All of a sudden, I jolted back to life and found myself at gunpoint by what looked like FBI officers. What had I done to deserve this?

Billy Ratcliffe (11)
High Tunstall College Of Science, West Park

THE GRIM REAPER

The Grim Reaper was normal once, he was called Billy Reaper, until this dreadful crime Billy committed. The last crime; murder, he did it to survive because his uncle was going to kill little Bill, but then Bill tasted the sweet release of anger towards him as the dagger sliced his throat. He did it more and more until the gods above punished Billy by trapping him in hell to become the eternal death that he bested from the people. The gods changed his name from Billy Reaper to the Eternal Grim Reaper!

Harry Ainslie (11)
High Tunstall College Of Science, West Park

MOTHER MADE ME

"I'm lonely, I can't do it anymore. What have I done? Help me," she whimpered, she was cold and quiet. She heard droplets of rain, the silence was loud.

"I'm sorry Father, it was Mother..." Pausing, she shivered, the cold pure breeze swept through her, the wet trees moved very slowly.

"I've had it. I can't live alone anymore. Yet I have no other choice to. I did it and I can't undo it. Oh, what I've done?" she questioned herself kneeling onto the rock-hard concrete.

"Mother made me, she's dead now... Oh, Father." She smiled like a psychopath.

Chloe Biddle (11)
Irlam & Cadishead Academy, Irlam

ALL FOR YOU...

"I did it to survive... I'm sorry my son." As I looked out across the podium I saw Alex and Toby (my workers) stood behind me... Silence. Eerie silence.

"I want to say thanks to everyone who voted-" Toby walked off but I didn't take much notice until... The ground started to violently shake. *Boom!* I fell to the floor, I couldn't move, I was paralysed. I saw the face of my co-worker Toby above me and people screaming in the distance.

"All for you... Father... all for you..." Suddenly he plunged his sword into my heart... announcing me dead!

Sammie Perry (11)

Irlam & Cadishead Academy, Irlam

HADES' SACRIFICE

"So, this is what it has come to," speaks Sage.
"Yes indeed," Hades replies. They begin to fight. Sage punches him in the stomach and Hades slaps him across the face. Hades is stronger than Sage, he won't win. Finally, Sage sinks down to the floor, full of pain. Hades grabs his sword and thrusts it into Sage's chest. Sage is dead. Suddenly, the darkness Sage sees disappears, he can see the light. He wasn't dead. He was alive! Hades has collapsed, he has used the last of his magic to transform his life to Sage's. Hades is now dead.

Kaysey Hudson (11)
Irlam & Cadishead Academy, Irlam

THE REAL STORY OF THE WOLF AND THE PIGS

Once the three little pigs destroyed the wolf's house. He was upset. He only wanted a home, so he tried to destroy the pigs' houses but was unsuccessful.

Maybe if I find materials somewhere, I can build a new better home, he thought. He started work laying brick, timber and mud, that did something. He tried three times but all building strategies failed because the mud was very weak. Then he finally completed it, but then out of nowhere three pigs arrived with weapons and knocked the house down. The wolf was like a sad statue. It was all over!

Liam Foster Spiers (11)

Irlam & Cadishead Academy, Irlam

HADES' VICTORY AND ZEUS' DOWNFALL

Hades, god of the underworld. He never wanted that job. Hades wanted to be king of the gods but that was Zeus' job. Can you believe it? Two people stood in his way... Hercules and Zeus. He needed to kill them, how hard could it be? For Hades... simple. As for that day he set off to kill the god and his son. Hades took Cerberus. In seconds, Cerberus ripped Hercules' head off and Hades took Zeus' head off. Finally Hades was king of the gods. Everyone was horrified. Shockingly, Hades made the gods' home a better place.

Tia Herring (11)

Irlam & Cadishead Academy, Irlam

VENOM VS BAKUGO

I'm sitting in my lair thinking. My plan is to kill the hero, Bakugo. Bakugo's powers explode out of his hands, he will be destroyed and I shall win.

I'm on my way to the battleground on Planet Symbiote to fight Bakugo. I've arrived, Bakugo seems to be here as well. We are both on opposite sides of the stadium. I go for the first smash and crush his insides but he explodes me with his hands. I have to strike his face. I smash his face. I win the fight and I am victorious.

"We are Venom!"

Riley Allen (12)
Irlam & Cadishead Academy, Irlam

THE TWISTED STORY OF BATMAN AND JOKER

Suddenly, the bell rang, something had been stolen. I dashed out of my cave so fast you couldn't say 'Batman'. The Joker... We glanced at each other as he got ready to fight. Crowds surrounded us like hungry lions. Joker smiled as I retrieved the diamond. Before I had time to punch him the cops took him away to be executed. Before the light got taken away from his eyes he said, "I didn't try to steal it, it was never me it was Harley, I hate you." I stood there frozen as he got taken away to die.

Nevaeh Price (11)

Irlam & Cadishead Academy, Irlam

PRISON LIFE

"Well... I'm going to have a day off from fighting and arguing with Sapnap and Karl. They keep coming into my cell with George, arguing that I should just... give up." As I walked out of my cell I put some clothes on, got some money to get food, until I accidentally bumped into Tommy and George at the cafe. Tommy looked nice but angry, he snatched my hat and I said, "Give it back Tommy, you don't need to do this." I snatched my hat and ran back to my cell with the food and ate it peacefully.

Olivia Carr (12)
Irlam & Cadishead Academy, Irlam

THE BEGINNING

I'd had enough! I was going to jump! Little did I know it was a tank for electric fish. Sinking deep into the water, I started to feel the power entering my body. Suddenly, the glass shattered and I gained consciousness. Once I had fully woken up that's when I realised. I was blue! Energy was flying out my body. Finally I was about to win. They all bullied me. They acted like I was never there. That was about to change! The lights switched off as I drained all of the energy. It was time I made myself known.

Vinny Atwal (12)
Irlam & Cadishead Academy, Irlam

PLANKTON'S STORY

Plankton is a notorious Bikini Bottom villain and top ten criminal. He has escaped every prison he has been in. He is microscopic compared to everyone else but despite his size, he still is a genius scientist. Plankton has been known to steal the Krabby Patty secret formula from the Krusty Krab but has never been successful in his heists to get all the money he needs. Things take a dark turn for Plankton when he used to be best friends with the person who is now his enemy, Mr Krabs, the owner of the Krabby Patty...

Joseph Bryan (12)
Irlam & Cadishead Academy, Irlam

FIERCE FLOODS

I never really belonged. Things were different. My friends were vanishing. All nature is disappearing. I must strike. I must begin. My plan is coming together. But who will I defeat? The entire human race. I shall flood the whole world. All humans will be gone forever. Who can beat me? No one. If anyone tries to ruin my plan they will be gone forever and ever. I must win. If not I will be defeated. That can't ever happen to me. I don't want to ever lose. Who will stop me from winning? I am a flood. I win.

Dhwani Patel (12)

Irlam & Cadishead Academy, Irlam

ANACONDA'S REVENGE

I never really belonged, nobody was ever kind to me and everyone attacked me in fear of being attacked themselves. I am known as the bad guy when I do things that I need to do to survive! Just because I have sharp teeth and slither around the forest does not make me a villain. When those heartless humans killed my whole family, I wanted revenge. I wanted to kill them!

Oh no! They're coming for me, they want to kill me too. I can't let that happen, I cannot fail them again like I did last year...

Corey Greenwood (11)
Irlam & Cadishead Academy, Irlam

POWERMAN'S PLAN

Hello! This is Powerman! I despise Superman. Here's why... we were inseparable until we were playing in the garden, he jumped, he flew. I got angry! I was jealous! *Now is my time to strike*, I thought, but I needed time to think, to plan. Now seventeen years later... he invited me to a party. I knew now was my time to strike. There I was poisoning his drink. "Muahahaha!" I laughed. The poison was strong. I'm sure he could smell it from the middle of the big, colourful dancefloor.

Kasey Smith (11)
Irlam & Cadishead Academy, Irlam

THE TRUE STORY

It hurts turning into what I despise. I wasn't always like this, I had a family, a job, a son... But, I couldn't resist anymore. My father gave me this gift, he said I would be normal... he lied. It turned me into a monster, made me turn, son and wife, I... ate them. I didn't get caught so I ran to America hoping for a new life, I thought wrong. The first night I slept on the street. A year later, I transformed into a monster. I didn't want to be born this way but it's my destiny.

Lucie Youd (11)
Irlam & Cadishead Academy, Irlam

DR OCTAVIUS' ORIGIN STORY

One day I (Dr Octavius) was working on electric arms to make me strong and powerful and make me feel good about myself. To make myself ruler of New York. I had finally made my arms and started to put them on. Then I was ready to plan world domination and to kill that goody-two-shoes Spiderman. I would be a part of history someday. My plan was finally completed and I was ready to begin the first step of world domination. All of a sudden Spiderman was there. Then I killed him and the rest of mankind.

James Prior (12)
Irlam & Cadishead Academy, Irlam

JOKER: ORIGINS

I never really belonged in this world, people judge me and they walk to the other end of the road when they see me. You see, when I was a kid I was an orphan, I was bullied for the way I looked, no one ever cared. As I got older, I thought that if people thought I was funny, they would forget how I looked, but no. They would embarrass me more and more. That's when I lost it. I would be hitting people, and robbing people until he came along. His name was 'Batman.' That is my origin.

Ethan Jones (11)
Irlam & Cadishead Academy, Irlam

THE BATTLE OF A CENTURY

The superhero act was all a lie, God is evil. We (Satan/Death) were kind people at first. God banished us from Heaven, tricked everyone else. So we planned revenge, after seven thousand years we were winning, we hoped. Zeus was away, (we didn't know that they knew we were coming.) Finally we were about to win but Zeus came, he defeated us, we weren't happy. We wanted to win but we were too weak so we trained and trained to the point where we could destroy a universe, we tried again.

Charlie Patterson (12)

Irlam & Cadishead Academy, Irlam

THE GREAT REVENGE OF MEDUSA

I did it all to survive, since the day I became this horrifying monster all I wanted was to live like a normal person again. I didn't want to take the life of innocent people every day, I wanted to be saved. I felt so helpless in this dimly lit, depressing cave, so alone. All of this suffering because of her... Athena. I had a new scheme to get back at her since my original one didn't work out. Just the thought that she is going to suffer the way I did puts a big grin on my face...

Emily Balde (12)
Irlam & Cadishead Academy, Irlam

UNSTOPPABLE

Many years ago my parents were killed by an alien. I was young so I didn't notice how bad it was but that alien lives in me, taking my body over. Sometimes it speaks to me but I can't figure out if I am hallucinating or not. It's real, all of a sudden, his head pops out of me and speaks to me. To this day I am most wanted in my country because of this alien. I call it Riot due to his anger and weapons he creates. I feel stronger and more powerful. We are now unstoppable.

Finley Ogden (11)
Irlam & Cadishead Academy, Irlam

LORD VOLDEMORT'S ORIGIN STORY

Once upon a time, I was only ten and I always felt left out and different. People started to bully me because of how I looked and had nobody backing me up, not even my parents. As I grew up I became a villain. I felt that I needed to get my own back on the people that were mean to me. That's what I did and I just kept doing this because it made me feel better about myself, my appearance. Harry Potter came to be. I planned to kill him but my plan backfired. I'm nothing.

Imogen Siddall (11)
Irlam & Cadishead Academy, Irlam

THE VILLAIN CHASE

It all started when one villain decided to be horrible to a hero and he wasn't very happy. So he made a plan to get the villain. He hunted the villain, when it got to the day, the hero had mixed emotions about what he was about to do but still wanted to get him. When he arrived at his location he went towards him and said, "Wanna battle?"
"Random question, but whatever." They both agreed that they were going to start to battle the next day.

Evie Mann (11)

Irlam & Cadishead Academy, Irlam

EVIL ELIZABETH

I really wanted to live in a really nice house with my husband but no, I got stuck in an old house with my husband and my daughter, when I didn't want kids. I've had it with this family, my husband Michael never has time for me anymore. Abbie's prettiness got on my nerves. I'm fed up with it all. I've tried to leave her at the shopping centre but her dad caught me. I was gonna have to go deeper. It became the day of the pageant. I poisoned her...

Isobe Rose Rowbotham (12)
Irlam & Cadishead Academy, Irlam

THE WOLF WANTED TO HELP THIS TIME

As she ran from me, I saw rocks ahead. So I started running after her to tell. I saw the look on her face as I ran. Suddenly, people surrounded me with guns and leashes. "Get the wolf!" was all I heard, so I had run away. I saw them chasing me so I ran faster, then cars and vans came too. So now I couldn't run. Suddenly there was a sharp pain, I had been shot. Slowly falling I knew I was gone, I knew I had left my wonderful family, because of them.

Hallie Sharples (12)
Irlam & Cadishead Academy, Irlam

TWISTED TALES

I still haven't forgotten that day when I was queen. It was a dream of a lifetime. I had everything I could imagine but then my sister took over, I was so mad. She made me an old little peasant. I worked on the farm and it was such hard work. But this one day I took over the whole world and my sister was a peasant. My dream was also to find a king but one day I felt bad for my sister and decided she could come and live with me. After all, I loved my sister.

Olivia Meehan (12)
Irlam & Cadishead Academy, Irlam

JAWS, THE TRUTH

It was a normal sunny day, kids on pool floaties, adults with babies. It was chilly down near the bottom of the sea. I rose up to feel the warm sun on my head, but instead, they caught me. They tied me up in a net and dragged me onto the irritating sand. I tried to bite and wiggle my way out, but it was no use. They stabbed me, punched me, until I was breathing no more. I was dead. They made me into soup and fed me to the parents of whose children I ate.

Molly Neill (12)
Irlam & Cadishead Academy, Irlam

JAWS: THE REDEMPTION

One day a beautiful girl was sunbathing on the beach. She decided to go for a swim, in the sea. Then a big killer shark came up to her and attacked her, he finished her off for dinner. The very next day Jaws was on the hunt for dinner but then he got caught in a net, panicking for help he managed to escape. Then the next day, still shocked about what happened, he decided to stop hunting everything except fish. He only did it for his friends and family.

Ysabel Brook (11)
Irlam & Cadishead Academy, Irlam

PLANKTON'S LIFE-CHANGING IDEA

There was a boy called Plankton and he had a plan to steal the secret formula of the next-door restaurant and wanted to get a lot of money. So he got his gear on and left to steal it, but it failed dramatically. As the alarm went off, straight away his plan failed, he realised that he could try to make things better by making it himself. Just making up his own, it was the best thing about it. He sold out every day, he's never been the same since.

Daniel Hind (11)
Irlam & Cadishead Academy, Irlam

VOLDEMORT BEFORE HARRY

As a child I was bullied for being poor and the way I looked, everywhere I went people would poke fun at me and call me names. So as I grew older I grew sick of it, I couldn't take it anymore. So I decided to turn to the dark side. I wanted people to be terrified of me, I didn't want my name to be spoken. So I trained in the arts of evil wizardry to show those people who are really useless and worthless. Don't believe me? Just watch.

Callan Atherton (11)
Irlam & Cadishead Academy, Irlam

REVENGE

I put on my black mask. I will commit the crime I have been planning all my life. I still haven't forgotten what he did. I will get my revenge. I drove to my location and when I got there I grabbed my lighter and a piece of wood. As I walked cautiously around his back garden, I heard his car pull into the drive, perfect timing! I picked the lock and opened the door. I grabbed the wood, set it on fire and watched the flame burst up...

Remy Budgeon (11)
Irlam & Cadishead Academy, Irlam

WOLVES

I never really belonged in the wildlife, all my family is dead thanks to these humans. I'm having a day off from trying to fight for my life. I'm never understood, (makes sense because I'm an animal) but all I have to do is act fierce just to get new friends. It's time to finally fight back, tomorrow I am plotting a plan to go down to the chicken flocks and set them free and cause chaos in town. I can't wait!

Grace Bowmer (12)
Irlam & Cadishead Academy, Irlam

DRACULA

Once there was a scary, pale, tall person whose name was Dracula. He was a mean, moody, horrible person, He killed people because he wanted to drink blood and rule the world. There was a rumour that he kidnapped a family and drank their blood until they died. He also tortured them so it was a slow painful death.

Emily Faulkner (12)
Irlam & Cadishead Academy, Irlam

VICTORIOUS VILLAINS

"Did you do it?"

"Do what?"

"Our dream, did it work out?"

"Your dream," they reach out for their waters, both thirsty.
"Mine is of carefree days, a wife, maybe kids, some sort of constant in this quagmire of uncertainty I've created." He set his glass back down.

"I don't want kids."

"Yes you do."

"I want-"

"I am aware. You want to splinter this world that has treated you so spitefully... You succeeded."

"We succeeded."

"No, again, it is you."

"I am you! We are the same!" Silence."You truly don't remember being me."

"I do. I simply regret it."

Rhea Gowda (13)
Rainham Mark Grammar School, Gillingham

REDEMPTION

What have I done... I can't do this anymore. But this world must pay for what it has done to me. But I can't. I have killed and destroyed so much. Can they forgive me? I can't think straight, I can't understand them. But I can help them, instead of hurting them. I can invent new products to help everyone! I will remake the world into, paradise with no problems. I have hundreds of products to help them. All I need is to sell them...

"Get this now, completely free!"

"Allows for all kinds of wonders..."

"Anyone?"

"Anyone?..."

"Hello?..."

"Hellooo?..."

William Adams (13)

Rainham Mark Grammar School, Gillingham

ORIGIN STORY

Nobody knows who I am. They only know me by name, and by the mistakes that I've made. Behind closed doors, my youth was unforgiving; nobody was ever there for me, and I wasn't doing particularly well in school. It was my family life that ravaged me - I've released my anguish through everybody else previously. Though it turns out I sabotaged my chances of gaining any company. Now I'm eighteen, all I want is someone that'll listen to me, since my parents don't currently. Wait. People say behaviour is instilled, right? Maybe it's time to plot something. Something they deserve...

Rhianna Morgan (14)
Rainham Mark Grammar School, Gillingham

WHO'S THE REAL VILLAIN?

I saw the life drain from his eyes, it was self-defence. He was trying to kill me, Bonifacio's greatest assassin. I tried to run and hide. Antoine Saverini was too good. After weeks of running, he finally caught up and pulled his sword from his sheath. "In pace requiescat," he murmured under his breath. Quickly, I dodged his deadly strike. I was horrified. Suddenly, my prayers were answered, his sword fell. Saverini's soul exited his body. I whispered,

"In pace requiescat," and fled to my home in Longosardo where I would hide. I would hide since they swore revenge.

James Martin (14)
Rainham Mark Grammar School, Gillingham

DOWNTIME

Tired and triumphant, I pulled into the driveway, my heart palpitated with excitement. The beast inside of me was out for blood; craved it, wanted it, needed it. But, of course, I must remain seemingly innocuous. The world sees me as sweet, charismatic if you please, but now it's time they taste my bitter revenge! I'm a sociopath, serial killer and cupcake entrepreneur. I own a cupcake stand that overlooks Lake Michigan. My victims are my secret ingredient. Today is my day off, no murder for me, just baking. The beast inside craves blood, he needs to be properly fed...

Phoebe Coulson (14)
Rainham Mark Grammar School, Gillingham

MOTIVATION

"You're a weak, petty, vulnerable child, grow up!" Dad screamed with fury.

Those few words have haunted me; still to this day as leader of police. Well Dad, this rough, tatty, yet relaxed town is mine now. Occasionally people arrive at my office, fists throbbing, smeared in blood and fury, obviously got in a fight (slightly common around here) expecting myself to actually care. Grow up people. This town smells of tobacco; that's funny. Why do I do this? I am police commissioner General Isaac and I do things for myself, not others, never Father.

Henry Gee (14)
Rainham Mark Grammar School, Gillingham

I AM NO HERO, I JUST HOPE I AM NO LONGER A VILLAIN

They taunted me, so I turned them into thoughtless, cannibalistic beasts (although they were monsters long before that). Then my only friend got bitten... When she turned into one, I was distraught; I couldn't even accept it. I spent the majority of the apocalypse I caused in my lab, concocting an antidote. The best I could do was cure the bitten before they turned. Feeling hopeless, I walked along an isolated road in despair, my failed antidote in hand. Suddenly, I discovered a bitten man laying in agony. I injected him, he twitched. Why did I have to destroy everything?

Sonika Aulakh (14)
Rainham Mark Grammar School, Gillingham

DRIPPING WITH POISON

I abhor my name. My name, Ichika Prisetsky Kamui. My parents didn't name me. I wonder why they abandoned me? I'm not insane or anything. No matter, I'm happy, all alone, without a hero. I do hope though, that they liked the bread I gave them. Filled with an almond-scented paste. Without any almonds. So sweet, their agony, like mochi. Mortals are honestly so jejune. Reminds me of my parents. I hate humans. I love all of you at the same time. Without sarcasm. I'll give you swiss rolls. I'm sure you'll like them. Swirled with my vitriol and cyanide.

Oluwadamilola Olatunji (13)
Rainham Mark Grammar School, Gillingham

ORIGIN STORY

After years of hanging around with rotten people, my life's ended up in misery. The sun is shining, people are out now, it's my time to shine. Creeping, crawling, breaking into an innocent person's house all for money. That's my lifestyle, sleeping, stealing and repeat. All thanks to some sickening people I hung around with, got me into doing evil things. Been doing the same old stuff for the past ten years. It's time I stand up and become the innocent guy I was decades ago. I'm going to move away and live the life I've always dreamt of.

Saffron Tyrone (13)
Rainham Mark Grammar School, Gillingham

ORIGIN STORY

Till death do us part, the promise I were to make to the king. My heart stolen, my loyalty none but true. Except that I'm penniless, some say impoverished. I mean we met, we danced, there was no reason to reveal my weakness. It would have stayed behind locked doors if Snow White hadn't snitched. A scoundrel she called me. Every ruthless word felt like my heart was being torn out. Days later no word from the king. Weeks later still no words. Months later my parents left home in disappointment. Only Snow White's loveless heart would satisfy me now.

Sophie Evans (14)
Rainham Mark Grammar School, Gillingham

BEHIND THE SCENES

Anger escaped him, leaving him feeling hollow. A shadow fell unnaturally across his face. Making him seem tall and imposing. He wore a mask, he no longer knew how to take off. Hiding his fear, his pain. He glanced at the ruins, his feelings hidden behind an impassive facade, structures, that stood tall and proud, lay crumbling, nothing but burnt-out shells. Bodies lay in the streets, he regretted it now, the destruction, the death. Light fell across his face, the sun just visible on the horizon. He walked forward till he reached the edge, one more step...

Ellen Passmore-Feast (13)
Rainham Mark Grammar School, Gillingham

MOTIVATION

The knife dropped heavily to the floor as his legs buckled, he followed, splashing in a pool of his blood.

"Why have you done this Father! What could cause you to end your own life!?" I too fell to the floor. I clenched my fists and screamed. That was some years ago but I have finally killed him. The last person who called him a coward. I gazed up as the heavens began to weep.

"I will be seeing you soon Father." I pulled a knife out and stabbed myself in the chest. I fell silently to the ground.

Joshua Abbott (14)

Rainham Mark Grammar School, Gillingham

AFTER EVER AFTER

I never say sorry... but this time I might have to. All the times you warned me, but I never listened. You were that mother figure for me, after you left, my life crumbled. My actions led me to poverty; homeless and fearful I could never fix my mistakes. I wish I could turn back time and feel safe in your arms, this gang life is dreadful. A constant fear of death. I scare everyone. I scare myself. I got myself too dragged up in crimes, I can't go back. And I'm sorry for that. I love you... remember that.

Erin Saunders (13)
Rainham Mark Grammar School, Gillingham

MOTIVATION

I had permanent scars, in my mind and on my body. After years of suffering and pain, I finally feel that I can be free. Now that he's gone. I never knew my mother, all I have of her is one small picture of her that sits beside me at night. Every day when I came home I was in constant fear of being hit and punished for no reason at all. He had been hitting me for as long as I can remember, my childhood was sad and painful. That's why I am who I am... a serial killer.

Charles Firth (13)
Rainham Mark Grammar School, Gillingham

WHO'S THE REAL VILLAIN?

Not for the first time in my life, murder, I am accused of. I am not the villain. I am the hero! Here lay I, on the streets I live. No family, no friends, no name. Unknown I am. Top of the wanted list I may be, but why you ask? You will see... Back to that night, there was a fight and now I lay here with a fright. I was walking my dog, when two men there were, one with a gun and one with a wound. Yes, I did save the poor man, but accused I am.

Kieran Crofts (13)
Rainham Mark Grammar School, Gillingham

RUSSIAN DOLLS

In the mortuary, the body was hollowed with care, the stitches, neat and hardly noticeable; a second corpse concealed inside.

"Just writing a handover note," I said, strolling into the office.

"Sam's left-handed. You're using your right."

I grinned. "Silly me. I was doing so well. My dear twin was so weak."

"You should be in the hospital."

"I should, but the nurse was so pushy, ironic I pushed her over the edge. However, your vigilance will cost you." This is such fun!

"You couldn't. Where would you hide the body?"

"Well... I do like Russian dolls."

Jenny Conyers (13)

The Martin High School, Anstey

GLOOMY GRAVEYARD TROUBLE

It's night-time. Fifty people gather together in a cemetery as someone has sadly died. The air is cold and gloomy. All of a sudden, strange noises ring around them. No one knows what's going on. Then, five people die out of nowhere. Everyone starts panicking. They head towards the exit, when all of a sudden, mist covers the whole place and a man with a hockey mask appears. He says,
"You're going to die!" Then, everyone starts dropping down. Gunshots ring around. After three minutes, everyone's dead, and the killer has disappeared into the dark, gloomy mist.

Aidan O'Donoghue (13)
The Martin High School, Anstey

THE JOKER'S REVENGE

Finally, I was about to defeat Batman. Entering his house, I was ready to kill this horrid man once and for all... *Bang!* He was dead. I was ready to take over Gotham City. A few days later, rumours circulated that Batman was dead. therefore, on Friday thirteenth, I sneaked around Gotham with blankets of darkness covering me. After I'd painted some buildings in purple and green I was about to head home, until an officer appeared. "What are you doing?" I didn't respond. *Bang!* On the man's dead body I wrote in blood: 'The rumours are true'.

Oscar Jones (12)
The Martin High School, Anstey

VAMPIRE BEST FRIEND

It was a new year at school. There were loads of new people. One was a vampire. Nobody knew them. The vampire's name was Elizabeth. She became friends, well best friends, with the popular girl called Karen. One night Elizabeth went round Karen's house. Karen hurt herself, she was bleeding. The blood attracted Elizabeth. She couldn't control herself. So she grabbed Karen and started sucking the blood out of her finger. Elizabeth wanted more. She leaned in and started sucking her neck. She was done so she wiped her memory and dumped her in the woods. Karen was never found.

Poppy Kinton (12)
The Martin High School, Anstey

DEATH'S RELUCTANT FOLLOWER

My name is Jenny, but they don't know that. To them, I am just death. My colleagues enjoy the endless suffering of others, I just experience an enveloping cloud of guilt. I hate this! Oh, another victim... What happened to this poor soul? My goodness, this child was brutally murdered. I can't let this one perish. I will give him a second chance at life. Goodbye child, love once more... What's happening!? Why do I have angelic wings, and see heavenly light?

"You have done a good deed, you're now an angel. You are now the pristine embodiment of me."

Harrison West (12)

The Martin High School, Anstey

THE GRINCH WHO ACTUALLY STOLE CHRISTMAS...

It was Christmas Day, the day my plan would come into play. Stealing Christmas. I started one by one going to each and every house. Nobody had realised I had stolen every horrible child's presents.

"The last house," I said to myself. As I walked in I noticed that traps were set everywhere. I had managed to steal all the presents though. I headed to my home where I stashed all the children's presents.

"I have done it." I let out an evil laugh. The cries of little children the next morning fueled my laughter and energy... Christmas stolen...

Alfie Gray (13)

The Martin High School, Anstey

THE STALKER

"She's dead," I said as I broke out in uncontrollable laughter. I've always wanted to kill someone, as she lay there stone dead I gazed upon her glistening blue eyes. "Sorry darling," I whispered. I was completely in love with her, I'm surprised she didn't notice something was up, like someone had been following her for the past two weeks.

I heard a screeching noise in the distance, it was a siren. I turned the dagger onto myself and plunged the shiny blade into my heart. This way, me and my beautiful bride could be together once more.

Kye Easingwood (13)
The Martin High School, Anstey

AND PEOPLE SAY I'M BAD

Bang! Gunshots rang around the room, the back door swung open, a large man dressed in black entered. At this stage of my life, I had never experienced violence. Because of the racket my dad came bursting into the room, pistol raised, *Bang!* My father fired. Moments after he fired the windows around me shattered. A hail of bullets flew at my dad, all striking him in various places in his body. As he dropped to his knees, blood was spewing everywhere. He fell limp. Men entered the room, a man dressed in white said, "Take Bruce now." My heart dropped.

Louis Proud (12)
The Martin High School, Anstey

PADLOCK

All my life I've wanted to carry on my dad's mission, to take over the world! I wanted to carry it on so he would be proud. But he told me there was one problem, it was something like Mufis. Suddenly, *bang! Bang! Bang!* But that time it wasn't outside as it echoed through the tunnel. Then again, *bang!* Black smoke filled the atmosphere and someone entered the room.

"I'm Mufis." But when he said it he didn't seem confident. I replied saying,

"I know who you are looking for, he's not here, I'm Padlock!"

Dylan Roberts (12)
The Martin High School, Anstey

THE DOWNFALL

I marched into Dimchester with my henchmen towards the Dimchester capital. This was my opportunity to take over. "Henchmen attack!" They charged, slaughtering and destroying anyone or anything in their path. Then I saw him, the last Avenger coming to stop me, but there wasn't any hope I was already taking over. As soon as I could reach him with my grabber I did. I pulled him in, squeezing his throat before he shot me with his laser and broke free. As quick as light my henchmen surrounded him crushing the last Avenger into the ground. I had finished him.

Thomas Little (13)
The Martin High School, Anstey

WHAT HAD I DONE?

Hazy, I lifted my head off the cold ground. My bloodied hands on the autumn leaves. I hoisted myself up. The dark, foggy night stared back at me. I didn't feel real. Faint, almost. Dissociated. Why? Why was I here? I couldn't remember... anything? I stood up and turned around. My childhood home? The place 'full of lovely memories', the place that housed my childhood; was abandoned...? I ran towards it,
"Mum? Dad?" I wanted to feel a warm hug again, one last time. Oh, what, Mum...? Dad? I looked at my hands once again. What had I done...?

Ksenija Bolc (13)
The Martin High School, Anstey

TRICKED!

Help!
Sprinting through the dreary melancholy forest breathing heavily, taking a glimpse behind me, a dark figure stares at me. This is excessive to handle, this is ghastly. Sprinting through hedges, he starts to catch up. I start to worry even more until I stop. All he says to me is, "I am a vampire, I have been hiding and running my whole life because no one accepted me. So help me please." He looks bleak and has no expression on his face and suddenly he grins.
Oh no!
"Help me please!" I've been lured into his trap. Help!

Alana Mason (12)
The Martin High School, Anstey

TWO WRONGS DON'T MAKE A RIGHT!

"And where do you think you're going!"
"To end you and your mess."
Deadeye planted a set of bombs around the centre of the city. Deadeye was the hero and was about to frame his arch-nemesis, Ultima. The bombs were set and Deadeye lined up a shot to blow the charges. Then Ultima entered his vision and realised what he was doing. Ultima was releasing them and setting them somewhere else. His goal was to eliminate the mayor of London. Deadeye knew what he did was wrong so he went to stop Ultima. But it was too late. *Boom!*

Austin Willson (13)
The Martin High School, Anstey

THE NIGHT WALK

I didn't know what I was doing. It felt like I had no control over my body. Before I could tell what I was doing I swung the plank of wood. I didn't know I was holding it. The man fell to the ground, I had no emotion. Finally, I was about to walk away without a care. A police officer stopped me. I asked them, "Why did you stop me?"

They replied, "Because you attacked an innocent man."

"Did I?"

"Yes you did and it isn't the first time."

"What do you mean? I was just on a walk..."

Olivia West (13)
The Martin High School, Anstey

GUILT

I did it for the mere seconds of pleasure, there wasn't any other benefit. Yet the guilt never caught up to me, not until today. He was limping, dragging his daughter. I could see the fear written in her eyes. The pure emptiness of fear consumed the natural blue they once were. Then it sparked inside me, a morbid heat of temptation arose inside me. I lunged forward, dragging her off of her father's grip, the screaming stopped, the seconds of pleasure faded almost immediately. He stopped running and turned. Just to find himself grasping one loose limb.

Alexander Down (13)
The Martin High School, Anstey

BE MINE

Haha, darling you must stay mine. Okay...? Your blood, it glides so elegantly down my knife... Why did you go? You're never going to leave again. Will you? The glowing rain outside. This moment, how calming it's so beautiful... Don't leave. Never! Never again. Your blood is so warm it tastes so sweet. The only person you'll ever love is me, that is all I am living for, that is my purpose in life. Please love me forever. Please just be mine... Allow me to repeat. Darling be mine. No. You are mine. Darling stop your tears, you're mine.

Ryuji Neal (12)
The Martin High School, Anstey

LIFE FINDS A WAY

The T-rex was loose. Power in the park was shut down as the lights clicked off one by one in the lab. I scrambled to navigate the wall of flashing buttons and switches for the master power switch. Dr Michaels' voice crackled through my radio at a million words a minute, his voice trembling as sheer terror set in. I heard a tyrant's roar as it ripped its fence to shreds. Dr Scarlett made her way down to the main power room as the systems wouldn't reactivate. Suddenly, Dr Michaels' voice cut out, drowned by the monster's battle cry...

Will Shaw (13)
The Martin High School, Anstey

THE ORIGIN OF THE SILENT KILLER

On a perfectly normal day, there was a rainstorm, well I thought it was a normal day. I decided to switch on my TV. Everything went silent, I tried to call my mum and dad but they didn't answer. Suddenly my TV turned on and the news said,
"A tragic accident has happened, Alan and Mary Butcher have died." I went silent. "The police have informed me, that they have been murdered." I ran to my grandma and grandad.
Two years later...
The murderer has been set free, now I seek revenge as 'The Silent Killer'!

Alex Ashfield (12)
The Martin High School, Anstey

RED

I did it to survive. I understand why anyone else would view me as being in the wrong, but they never listen to the 'Villain's' story. I stand here now, alone, yet if I'd never killed her, she would've killed me first. She thought I didn't know her plan, yet I've known since we were young. She never had been good at keeping secrets. It's funny really; I had always had a fear of blood, yet the red-dyed sheets made me feel euphoric. Maybe I've done a good thing. Her favourite colour had always been red, after all.

Evelyn Stott (13)
The Martin High School, Anstey

THE HUSKS AND THE GIRL

She dived into the church, barring the door. As if that could stop me. I rushed under the door, time to play... I slammed the shutters, blew out the candles, ripped the tapestries and swooped. My bony arms cracking as I grabbed her. The pathetic being wriggled, "Bury your sins and pray they never rise!" I screamed and threw her to the floor. I sensed another human. I pinned him to the wall, tears rolling down his face. I snapped his neck. Back to the girl. I grabbed her, "Give me it and I will kill you quickly and painlessly."

Jessica Wragg (13)
The Martin High School, Anstey

THE MAN AT THE DOOR!

One gloomy night the graveyard gates creaked open and a man in all black approached the church. The man had a pointed hood, all black, the hood was up. The night got later and the man was now knocking at a house door, as laughing children approached. The kids backed away and the mum came over to ask what the matter was, the man said, "Be prepared for death."

The family was now asleep and the man climbed through the window and upstairs. He slashed the family's necks. The dad pulled up outside and went in. His family was dead!

Sophie Penhaligon (12)

The Martin High School, Anstey

NO ESCAPE

The children wailed as they crawled on their knees, quivering, leaving blood trails and sombre memories. The same old man was back again... I ran but his voice echoed along the walls of torture, "You can run but you can't hide." He smirked, licking his lips. He bent down, I saw the knife drop. A fresh kill. I threw myself at the man screaming for help. My eyes filled with tears. I reached for the knife and slashed his throat. He dragged me by my leg with the last strength he had and took me to the dungeon. *Lock clicks.*

Lily Carter (12)
The Martin High School, Anstey

THE KILLER GHOST

Sneaking around the town finding my next prey. My ghostly self stumbled along the Queen's palace, I floated through the walls. Little kids were running away, I thought they saw me. I found a servant and went in for the kill. Blood dripped everywhere all around the walls.

"I can't be caught."

I floated into the Queen's room, I went to kill her, just as I arrived she shouted,

"Stop! I can see you!" I was done for. "I will report this you evil monster, you will never get away with this!"

Lillie Sutherington (12)
The Martin High School, Anstey

NO ONE SHALL GET IN MY WAY

I sat in my dead father's chair, waiting for someone to find out and come stumbling from fear. I sighed, it felt like forever.

"How boring," I groaned. However, my luck increased as a man frightened to the very marrow of his bones, screamed out, "All of them, dead, even your father!" I smiled, I did it, I fooled them. I let out a psychotic laugh, walking to the gun on the floor, I needed to kill him too. I made sure the gun was loaded by shooting at the wall. *Bang!* It shot. Turning, I pointed the gun...

Vanessa Koscielniak (12)
The Martin High School, Anstey

FOREVER MINE

She said our love was tainted, hoped I'd replace her but she was special. I'd left her for a moment to think about her actions, I collected my thoughts. It was then I knew that this was the only way to ensure she'd be mine. She could hear my footsteps, her breathing slowed. This was a sign. I began repeating,

"I'm sorry." I didn't mean it but she had to know I cared. I gouged her heart out, blood dripped from the sockets, it still beat in my hands. She was finally completely untouchable. Forever mine.

Lola Wright (15)
The Martin High School, Anstey

DEATH! THIRST FOR BLOOD

The thirst for blood is immense. It shadows my body forming an ominous aura around me. I just have a duty to slaughter the feeble. Justice must be served to the innocent. Those who pay their respect to the dead; I must kill them so they are with their fallen loved ones. My favourite fatality was when I decapitated the victim then slit their limbs into fragments. After this great phenomenon occurred, I realised I had murdered my own species. This made me broken even more, now I am even more bloodthirsty and villainous. For I am death.

Lucas Armstrong (13)
The Martin High School, Anstey

THE LIFE OF A PSYCHO AFTER ESCAPE

I was finally free from that hell hole. I was emerging ever closer towards a run-down pub, I entered stealthily. I aimed a glass bottle right at the bartender's head, he was unconscious. I stole both his clothes and his keys for a Focus in the distance. I could hear wailing sounds of sirens edging closer and closer to me. I frantically hopped into the Ford Focus and zoomed off. The pills I had taken before I escaped the asylum were finally kicking in. The car was turning to the left then to the right then *boom! Crash...*

Elljay Layshley-Wardhaugh (12)

The Martin High School, Anstey

MORE THAN DARKNESS

As the battle was ending, the strain grew larger. I thought I was going to lose. But alas, in the final moments, I ended this war forever. Within minutes, Gotham City descended into a cruel and unnerving darkness. After a few days, I grew bored. I began to wander the city. The bare streets felt almost disturbing, as if I had woken more than darkness. I began to hear voices. Moments later, I saw the pale and monstrous victims of my victory. I had killed their hero. They had soulless, empty eyes. They walked slowly towards me. I ran.

Woody Payne (12)
The Martin High School, Anstey

CINDERELLA'S GLASS SLIPPER

After the evil sisters found out me and the prince got married I turned them into my slaves. They had a taste of their own medicine. Day in day out they cleaned until their whole bodies ached. They made my outfits till there were perfect. One day I found them looking into my drawers full of jewellery, I walked on my tiptoes making sure the floorboards didn't creak, I grabbed their hair and bashed them together, they fell. I pulled their legs down to the basement and stabbed them with my glass slipper, blood was everywhere...

Ayla Ward (13)
The Martin High School, Anstey

VICTORY.COM

Finally, I was about to win. I impaled yet another one of the vermin's men, pinning them to a wall. I drew closer, the stench and pure hatred I held towards him beckoning me onwards. I threw a katana, slicing through three people all at once. I was almost there. He entered the room, running towards me he made a feeble attempt to strike me down. I dodged, easily tearing off his head, the scent of blood filling the air. I took in my accomplishment until finally, I tossed the remains of his mangled body aside, I had killed him.

Harry Butcher (13)
The Martin High School, Anstey

EVERYBODY'S A KILLER IF YOU PUSH THEM FAR ENOUGH

The date was 31st October, Halloween. It all started in a maze. It was meant to be a fun, friendly time with family but it wasn't what I thought. We were in the middle of the maze. Everything seemed normal. Until we came to the centre. There was a scarecrow standing in front of us holding a knife. Somehow the face looked familiar. We took one step forward and it twitched. We moved two steps forward, it grabbed my mum and stabbed her to death. I found out it was Dad. Everybody's a killer if you push them far enough...

Mia Witherington (12)
The Martin High School, Anstey

THE MISUNDERSTANDING

I still haven't forgotten about what happened in the incident. I wanted to conquer the world. I didn't really belong to a family; both my parents died. I blame it on the home I was in after the accident. The people there were malicious, I had no choice but to become evil. That place made me feel mistreated and mentally disturbed. It made me want to get revenge. When my plan was in motion, I knew I was ready. I knew this process would take time, I just had to be patient. Finally, I was about to finish, but then...

Rohan Verma (13)
The Martin High School, Anstey

OBSESSED

"Dogs, dogs, dogs! Get them out of my head!" They were making me mad. It had been six years since they escaped me. My coat mannequin still lay bare. I still wander the streets for the evil beasts. On one of my walks, there was movement down the dark and twisted alley. I crept down, "I have got you now!" To my horror, it wasn't them but a cat. I squeezed it tight, holding it up to my chest.
"Ahh you're beautiful aren't you? But you would be even more beautiful as a coat..."

Abigail Newton (12)
The Martin High School, Anstey

THE EXPERIMENT

I still haven't forgotten the screams that echoed in my ears as I watched, helpless. The sound of a knife cutting through flesh made my skin crawl. My eyes shot open, my body shuddering with grief. The faint beep and clean white walls reminded me of where I was. The noise of muffled talking soothed me. I tried to make out what they were saying. I jumped as the door opened, and a nurse appeared. She placed down some sharp tools on the table and left. My hands began to shake as I eyed them, and I smiled in revenge...

Sky Spicer Hadley (12)
The Martin High School, Anstey

THE UNLOVED

My parents were drinkers and smokers, they'd argue every day. They used to bring their friends round to bully me. Until they abandoned me outside a church. I was taken in by an orphanage. I was put in a black room with a rusty bed. I would sit there day after day wanting revenge. One day I escaped and went into hiding, I hid behind bin bags every day. My plan was to murder people hoping that one day I would have killed my parents. I started the killings around the area and no one could ever stop me killing...

Dave Muton (12)
The Martin High School, Anstey

THE TAKEOVER

I had finally done it, I defeated Batman. Everybody in Gotham City was shocked when it was on the news. Until they heard that Robin was still alive. That's the only hope they had. I was laughing because they didn't know that I already had him. I could see the tears running down his face as he was tied up to a chair. I got to the news building and shut it down. Then I recorded a video of Robin and projected it on all the buildings and every TV. Gotham City was petrified and Robin didn't want to die.

Harry Jaques (13)
The Martin High School, Anstey

FAMILY TRADITION

I stabbed someone, the blood was squirting out. It reminded me of my childhood. How my father was holding a knife and how the blood was oozing out of the dead bodies. The knife was trickling with blood. They screamed and screamed, then there was sudden silence. My father had a psychotic laugh. I stood in front of a mirror and I saw my father, I was a replica of him. I carried on doing my business. Now I am going to be in the newspaper. My father would be so proud of me. The family tradition shall never die...

Julia Wojtkiewicz (12)
The Martin High School, Anstey

MYLING

It was a dull, soundless night. I had met up with my friend, we had intended to catch the international myth of the Myling. The child nightmare. We ran the dreary track of the hallows of the woods, that was until we noticed a vibrant orange flame that symbolised the presence of the Myling. We ran to the scene. To our surprise, it was a crimson-red house, the colour of dry blood flushed the house. I had never intended on killing my best friend. It was just the wrong moment. I guess the so-called myth is true.

Meg Ainge (13)
The Martin High School, Anstey

THE DEATH OF BATMAN

Boom! I blew up a car near me, a man's destroyed bloody body landed next to me, I sprinted to my Joker funhouse, where dead, crippled people lay. My traumatised prisoners watched as they went into insanity, while they were starved and tortured. I heard a creak, it must be Batman. I got my crowbar with bloodstains on it. I stood on the polished green door as the Dark Knight walked in. I dropped from the door and hit him between the eyes. Finally free, until I saw a dark shadow behind me...

Marley Onions (12)

The Martin High School, Anstey

DAY OFF

I'm having a day off from plotting a fiendish plan. On my days off I chill in my lair in my onesie and watch The Grinch whilst eating onion-flavoured popcorn. I like to play my Nintendo Switch, Mario Kart is my favourite because I love cars as well. My girlfriend comes round and we play exercise games, so we have fun and burn calories at the same time. We love doing exercise. I take a ridiculously hot bath and get in my towel made from dog skin and put Netflix on the TV, with my dog Silly Sally.

Cassidy Roberts (12)
The Martin High School, Anstey

THE STRANGER

Dave was rummaging through boxes trying to find new clothes and old toys for his expected child. His wife (Mary) was lying down reading a book to cure her boredom. She heard the door open, she thought it was her mum coming to check on her, or it could have been her son coming home from school. Dave shouted from the attic, there was no response. Mary had a perfect view of the landing. A man wearing a black hoodie, a white mask and Nike joggers stared at Mary. She was in shock. A weapon was drawn...

Joseph Quinn (12)
The Martin High School, Anstey

THE GRIM REAPER

I am the notorious Grim Reaper. But I am misunderstood. My owner controls me. He is always watching, he is always listening. I used to have a family and friends but I was poached from my life all because of my owner, God. People all around the world worship and pray to him but it is all a lie. I cannot disobey him or else he will erase me and replace me. I only do the things I do to survive and protect good people from my fate, from God's wrath. But people will never know the truth, the lies.

Taylor Leuty-Smith (12)
The Martin High School, Anstey

EVERYONE'S A KILLER IF YOU PUSH THEM HARD ENOUGH

I stood over his lifeless body.

It all started when Jack White came up to me and slipped me a note, 'Imagine wanting to be a surgeon freak'. I knew he was going to make my life a living hell. For the next year he tormented me, he even showed up at the library a couple of times. Once, he rang my phone and left me a voicemail saying if I didn't stop going to the library after school that he would kill Mrs Smith. That was the last straw, someone needed to teach Jack a lesson...

Shylah Johnson (12)
The Martin High School, Anstey

THE TARGET

The scope was aligned with the target I had been paid too much to turn down. A lot of money had been owed to people. I stopped, suddenly feelings of hatred flooded my mind. The source of where these came from, my father. He had to die, he was forcing me to do his dirty work for money. I knew where his location was, so finding him wouldn't be the hardest part, killing him would be. I rushed over and set up. Change had to be made, for real this time. The shot was fired, it was almost over.

Daniel Norman (12)
The Martin High School, Anstey

THE CREATION OF DEATH

One midnight, it was raining in the rundown lab when he was creating it. Moments later it came to life, it grabbed a small knife on a desk next to it and killed the person who created it. It ran out of the lab and ran into the city. It started killing people but after a while, it stopped, people thought it finally died but it didn't. It was hiding in the woods near the city. But one person knew it was alive and wanted to kill it after it killed his family. He put traps in the woods...

Tyler Barclay Wakefield (13)
The Martin High School, Anstey

I DID IT TO SURVIVE...

I could hear my heart thumping like it was in my head, I panicked and hid. The resentful security guards flew past. I sprinted back to the codes. I swiftly put the code in. *Error*, what was wrong? I did it again. *Error*, I tried one last time hastily as I could hear security hustle down the halls. "1420", it was incorrect. I had been working on this for months but it was thrown away in seconds. The guards surrounded me, I had no choice I had to do it...

Olivia Hands (13)
The Martin High School, Anstey

BROTHER

I never really belonged in this world. You see, when I was younger, me and my brother were never treated nice, we were beaten by our parents and bullied. One day, my brother was killed by the bullies in the park, he was beaten up, but they didn't care, not even our mum or dad. Now I sit in my home, still planning to kill all of the people that killed my brother like the bullies and my mum and dad and nobody will get in my way. No matter how long it takes, I will get revenge...

Archie Lloyd (13)
The Martin High School, Anstey

HANGING BODIES

Was my mind playing tricks on me? The hanging bodies in front of me said otherwise. Blood dripping from their fingers and toes. All I could focus my eyes on was the white powder next to me. My only thought was, I was framed, framed by white powder, forcing me to go crazy! I was sure to be caught with this many bodies in my basement. I felt my face turn pale. Guilt. Guilt had taken over. Hooks piercing the skulls of my victims. I couldn't take it anymore. I was a serial killer.

Jess Hodgkinson (13)
The Martin High School, Anstey

ALL IN A DAY'S WORK

As I walked into my lair I let out my favourite most evil laugh. I went and put my onesie on and took my SD card out of my Go Pro Hero 6 and uploaded it to my TV and watched my most beautiful murders of the day. I watched myself cut The Shard down with a chainsaw.

"Ping kill count 690." I celebrated my most murders with a hot-blooded chocolate. So I pierced a hole in my skin and let my blood squirt into my cup and then I added a bit of chocolate powder and water.

Gene Wright (12)
The Martin High School, Anstey

A MATCH MADE IN HELL

The floor cracked open. The violent screams were like music to my ears as I rose from the fiery pits of Hell. I looked to the sky, there she was. The one I wanted. The one who needed to perish. It was the angel. I edged closer to her, she edged closer to me. It had worked. I had control of her through the power of my mind. I grabbed her arm and only then did she realise who I was. She panicked but I just laughed. I let go. She fell down to Hell. This was my perfect victory.

Freddie Elkington (13)

The Martin High School, Anstey

THE TRAP

I did it to survive, I felt that I was in a room without an exit but I told myself I would get out... *But why am I here?* I thought to myself, I thought hard about it, then my father came into view, as I thought about my father my body began to... Feel angry, I didn't know why, then it hit me. It was him. That monster, no, that reincarnation of evil. With the evil inside of me building up I created something worse than my dad. Something horrifying...

Niall Farrell (12)
The Martin High School, Anstey

THE KILLER

On a dark gloomy night, there was a noise coming from downstairs. I went down to investigate and *bang!* The door slammed right in my face. But I was home alone so nobody should've been there with me. I tried the door again and the door was still locked. How was I meant to escape? Soon after I gave up. I looked into an old mirror, I saw a murderer standing behind me with a black shiny gun. Then they stood so close to me and then pointed it at me...

Grace Sylvester (13)
The Martin High School, Anstey

HOW VILLAINS ARE MADE

Instead of being taught kindness and caring, I was taught violence and stealing in public. I was expected to talk to people but in reality, I was the one to argue. My parents wanted me to accomplish one goal and that was to be the worst I could be. In my childhood everything I owned had to be bad in some way, the books I read involved killing, which I found quite thrilling. I never had toys like puzzles or bikes, all that I had was guns and knives.

Curtis Blunt (12)
The Martin High School, Anstey

THE MYSTERIOUS MAN

I went to my farm and I suddenly heard a colossal bang!
"What was that?" I said to myself. The barn. I heard
screeching coming from the mammoth barn. A mysterious
man whipped out a knife attached to a chain. Straight away
he threw it at me. I had to react quickly so I jumped out the
way and grabbed the closest thing to me to throw at me. It
was a sky blue wrench. It hit him and it landed on his skull. It
was the end for him.

Callum Shokar (12)
The Martin High School, Anstey

MY HIDDEN SIDE

I remember standing in my room and the next thing I knew I was surrounded by corpses, it had happened again. I felt strangely proud, I'd lost all control. I just flip and all my suppressed anger comes out, what happens after that is a blur. There's a side of me that has these urges to kill. The screams of my victims convince me to not stop. It wants me to harm the people I love and I can't go on like this...

Caitlyn Timson
The Martin High School, Anstey

Young Writers Est. 1991

YOUNG WRITERS
INFORMATION

We hope you have enjoyed reading this book – and that you will continue to in the coming years.

If you're a young writer who enjoys reading and creative writing, or the parent of an enthusiastic poet or story writer, do visit our website **www.youngwriters.co.uk**. Here you will find free competitions, workshops and games, as well as recommended reads, a poetry glossary and our blog. There's lots to keep budding writers motivated to write!

If you would like to order further copies of this book, or any of our other titles, then please give us a call or order via your online account.

Young Writers
Remus House
Coltsfoot Drive
Peterborough
PE2 9BF
(01733) 890066
info@youngwriters.co.uk

Join in the conversation!
Tips, news, giveaways and much more!

 **YoungWritersUK** 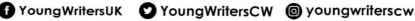 **YoungWritersCW** 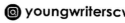 **youngwriterscw**